Radiant as Rapeseed

Radiant as Rapeseed
Jennifer Sakamoto

ISBN-13: 978-1-948712-65-1

© 2021 Jennifer Sakamoto

Weasel Press
Lansing, MI
https://www.weaselpress.com

to hertz sensei
for teaching me
the definition of poetry

to my brother
for treating me like blood

and to maria
for everything else

Contents

i

ii

iii

iv

Radiant as Rapeseed

Jennifer Sakamoto

i

villanelle vi

she's so beautiful her aura noblesse
even the shadow of her voice i need
her no so sweet it's practically yes

the birthmark atop her collarbone i obsess
how vulnerably she breathes when she doesn't concede
she's so beautiful her aura noblesse

her screams when i enter hold perfect stress
she knows how to make me powerful indeed
her no so sweet it's practically yes

the captivation of credulous and lovely her finesse
her pulse as radiant as rapeseed
she's so beautiful her aura noblesse

petite picturesque powerless
perfect prey on her veins i read
her no so sweet it's practically yes

how satisfying it is to conquer than be gifted ingress
clenching something so fair till it crumbles and beads
she's so beautiful her aura noblesse
her no so sweet it's practically yes

gogyohka xv

i was raped
i believe you

thank you but stating fact
and asking for your belief
are two different things

untitled i

was it nighttime
did you tell anyone where you were
why were you alone with him

but didn't you have a crush on him
did you send mixed messages
what were you wearing

did you say no
did he hear you
was it clear
when you said no was it seductive

so you didn't say yes but you didn't say no right
don't you have a reputation of being a flirt
did you lead him on
isn't he saying it was consensual

who made the first move
how did he touch you
could you repeat that please
could you repeat that in more detail

are you sure you're remembering it correctly
did it feel good
could you repeat that please

if it truly was rape why didn't you fight back
why haven't you taken self-defense courses
why didn't you report it

why did you take a shower after
there are no witnesses right
do you have any proof
could you repeat that please

why do you keep putting yourself in these situations
why were you being woman
why were you breathing

oh i get it
it truly is
worth all of the trouble
than to simply believe me

logic

the only possible way
it would be my fault
is if you don't recognize it
for what it is
rape

but if it's not rape
then you wouldn't be blaming anyone

villanelle xviii

it hurts too much what pain is this
aftermath my dear
there is a way i promise

where is my pulse why is my body remiss
am i dead or is there more to fear
it hurts too much what pain is this

almost all of your life that night will kiss
though relief will not knock near
there is a way i promise

i want to scream but can't breathe in this abyss
my blood has no rufous my tears no clear
it hurts too much what pain is this

trust the stings the screams the stabs will dismiss
though they will never fully they will disappear
there is a way i promise

my stolen soul i miss
please tell me this'll be my darkest tear
it hurts too much what pain is this

there is a way i promise

untitled ii

eager to make a new enemy today
i sit opposite my counselor
i was raped
have you experienced people
not believing you yet
i kill eye contact and nod

i believe you
you believe me you believe me
based on what
based on evidence
or the evident lack of it
saying i was raped is just words
i could be lying

with calmness
she looks me up and down
the evidence is before me
the evidence lies in the words you say
and how you speak them
how defensive how skeptical how angry you are
is too raw to be an act

i break down and weep
after all i've gone through
i didn't know it was possible
to feel understood

i stand to leave
i don't want to see you anymore
i'll see you next week

untitled iii

i told you of my second abuser
i told you i was revictimized

you said you saw it coming
predicted it even
after all history repeats itself

why only now do you speak

untitled iv

when my best friend
catches me lost in thought
she knows what i'm thinking about
but knows not how to comfort me

it is in these moments
i wonder if she too is thinking
about anything
i wonder if her heart
feels anything
i wonder if it ever crosses her mind
to pick up a book
do some research
feel less answerless
i wonder if she's waiting
for me to guide her
point her toward an answer

if so then after all of the people
who didn't listen to or believe me
i have no energy left
to teach someone
the timing of taking initiative

love poem xx

my darling sun you rose today
as you do every day
everything begins with you
so how can i not be in awe

do you know how grateful
i am to you
do you know i should
wake up bowing east
do you know you saved me
of course you know
you're the sun

when i couldn't rise you did for me
when everyone left you never did
when i could only feel darkness
you blinded me with light
made sure i saw you
made sure i saw me

on the dusks you had to say goodbye
you first drew me your horizon
pronounced that though imaginary in line
your beauty is worth waiting
another day to see again

if you weren't lethal to touch
i would kiss you
kiss you for hours on end
till you rise again

you are not the moon nor the stars
you are my sun
i revolve around you

riddle viii

what's the difference between
someone who was raped yesterday and
someone who was raped a year ago

the former says i'm not lying
the latter says i'm telling the truth

untitled v

instead of simply comforting me
she makes sure i take note
of her i told you so
you never listen to me
why didn't you buy pepper spray
the first time i said to

i say nothing and in the silence
she senses she has spoken senselessly
she apologizes as she should
but there is no need

thank you
that's the most consideration
anyone has given me in months

what six-year-olds know

enomoto sensei smiles at her saturday scholars
in an attempt to get us excited
for the oxymoron that is word game

today we play unscramble
kento-kun volunteers as always
because he likes the smell of chalk
he scrambles pears p-e-a-r-s into sprea s-p-r-e-a

pears why didn't i guess pears
his totoro lunch bag
births them like a tree

instead of assessing possibilities
and unscrambling how the spare spear reaps
or pares
i see but one word and raise my hand
rapes

life continues normally for everyone
except enomoto sensei
she looks up from her cancam magazine
how do you know that word

what an odd question
i pause to think
my tongue ever so slightly
slips out between my lips for air
as it thinks too

ignorant of its weight and actual definition
i know the word like i know breathing
in the most innocent of melody i exhale
i don't know
i just do

untitled vi

mieko my inner child
torques my eyelids till i wake
where do rainbows get their crayons
if i eat a lot of lucky charms
will i become lucky or charming
do fish not like birds
because birds can fly and they can't

why do you look like me
but bigger
we're the same person sweetheart
you're a part of me

if we're the same person
why are we different
what do you mean
my face is normal
your face is always scrunched
you look like you're in pain
that's because i am sweetheart

that doesn't make sense
if we're the same person
why am i not in pain
because you don't yet know
you were abused sweetheart

yes i do i know
oh is that so
then how are you so happy
because i know when you're even bigger
you won't be in pain anymore
you'll be content
like me

how do you know that sweetheart
life's a process
your point being
just trust me

untitled vii

my good friend and her boyfriend
stay at my house for the weekend
despite knowing one
should be kind to her guests
i can't help but hand him a dirty look
every time she leaves the room

after our first dinner
he kindly clears the table
properly places the petunias
on the counter
the dishes in the sink

i stare at him in great disgust
whilst she's still in the room
not a one of us knows why

knowing i have dampened the evening
she takes a couple of sleeping pills
at the dining table
shames me with her walk up the stairs
and retires early
with no looks left to give
her boyfriend and i follow suit

an hour later nothing strange is seen nor heard
but my gut punches me
i rise to check on her

down the hallway i go
he stands atop her sleeping form
his index finger pulling down her skirt

he spots my shadow
with both evil and fear in his eyes
he grabs his jeans
runs out the backdoor

before doing anything
half-frozen i wonder
how i will tell her
how she will take it
how either of us
will be able to sleep tomorrow

my heart hates knowing
that though i prevented a raping
on this dark beautiful night
he will probably find
someone else's soul to take
before the turning of a calendar page

after all we survivors win battles
not wars

untitled viii

he enters her vagina
as if a human is not attached to it
in a few moments
when her soul is no longer hers
his actions will be accurate

at midpoint
she grows too defeated
to cry or scream
instead she pretends to like it

after all if you pretend
it was your idea
if you pretend
you chose to have sex
then it feels a little less like rape
now doesn't it

ii

moth catcher

a mother is beautiful
she hugs you
in her miraculous body
through both the bliss and sting
nine magical months bring

she raises you
teaches you manners
without her you are caveman
when the world you trusted parts
she sacrifices her life for your own

a mother is beautiful
if she truly is
a mother

dear mother
it's so hard to call you that
there were entire clocks
where we did not breathe the same air
the blood shared between us
wasn't ours for years

despite all of this missed time
you said you feel like
you've known me from birth
as if you've always had me

there are days i want to
pick up the phone to call you
just because
i have no questions to ask

nor no answers to give
i just want your voice

but it's too hard to call
it's too hard to call a mother
who isn't a mother
mother

they say if you
repeat a word enough times
it loses its letters
it loses its definition
this is true
as i've repeated the word mother
in search of one
too many times

sometimes i even read
the word mother in a book
and it has become so unrecognizable
i ask myself what does moth•er mean
is it a person who catches moths

i don't know what a mother is
but i know what a mother isn't
a mother isn't one who sees blindly
every time her daughter
shares a bed with her father
a mother isn't one who forever lives in denial
when knowing her daughter lost her innocence
before she was old enough to spell sex
a mother doesn't lie in court
to defend her sex offender of a husband
at the risk of losing her daughter

a mother
doesn't lose her daughter

can you please change who you are
entirely
because i need a mother
i want to talk to her
trust her enough to hug her
i want someone i can say i love you to

i want to pick up the phone to call you
but i want the person on the other end
to be a mother

signed
i can't say i'm your daughter

untitled ix

mieko and i go to the dentist
so she can have her first lollipop
in the waiting room
she flails her legs diagonally and sideways
as if she's never learned how to sit

do you wish to hold my hand sweetheart
why
after being abused
what pain left do i have to fear

untitled x

i've been trying to make myself
feel better for years
and in failing
i've learned this is not the way

after seeking and sought
there is nothing that can make this better
make the pain of the abuse better
it is too deep a grave to fill
to ever stand on level ground

the answer lies not in better
not in making the impossible breathable
but rather in defining where i start

i imagine earth to skin
grass and soil
contouring the curves of my feet
and from here
note i am standing on ground
able to be

untitled xi

i hesitate to call in sick
because who will believe me
after coughing and sneezing
in the same breath
my left limb pushes me to lift
i pick up the phone

the receptionist tells my boss
and she understands
in discreet shock
all i can feel is
how naive are you
to believe me

notes to devoted sitter

when mieko hides her vegetables
especially her watermelon
in her hollowed-out copy
of réti's modern ideas in chess
which she will
tell her a writer can't write
without the nutrition
that is watermelon

she will stare at you in blank gaze
know you are lying
then eat her portion
in gratitude of your put-forth effort

aside from vegetables
speak to her as you would an adult
she comprehends no other way
the more you use your imagination
whilst making a point like
sloths know the best parts in life
need no rushing to
the more she'll engage

when she debates you
over sleeping later
and wins
have her listen on loud
to her favorite audiobook
start after the intermission

when she smiles in chapter twelve
whilst eiji-kun speaks and his soul bleeds

hide your uncomfortableness
as its basis is inaccurate
she is merely soothed in noting
that in this lonesome world
there are others like her
who comprehend suffering in its depth

when she begins to blink blindly
have her bathe and brush her teeth
once in bed
birth a bedtime story
from your imagination
it can be magical or scary
no need to censor yourself
she'll love all words
so long as you speak them

when she sleeps in still serenity
then clenches her plush lion cub
too tightly in dreaming
there is a need to do nothing
merely sit near on call
know she is processing the pain
too penetrating for plain day
and by morn
less pain there will be

untitled xii

when i was six
my biological mother and i
saw a call for ransom on the news

i spoke but now wish i went silent
if i were kidnapped
would you pay my ransom

depends on how much
oh that makes sense

***

was it that i was too logical a child
or that the molestation taught me
my lack of worth all too well

i've thought it over and over and learned
i'll never know

untitled xiii

they tell me i'm lying
every day
and i am left
with no one to talk to
no one on my side
i am worn down

mieko doesn't see me for the exile i am
and is happy to sit next to me
did i cry wolf like they say
am i a liar
did i lie
i don't know whom to believe anymore

with experienced eyes
she looks into me
do you believe me

grammar

how can you warn me
don't get yourself raped
then blame me
when the deed is done
how is it my responsibility my fault
when it is not something i do
but rather something
that happens to me

go ahead and blame me
point fingers all you want
your words in point of fact
prove you wrong
as even grammar knows the truth

untitled xiv

as fellow writing club members
critique my poem
i note the new member five seats over

i've smelled the scent of silence before
but he so sharply speaks wordlessly

upon club dismissal
he applies his logic to the topic of rape
turns to a listener
and speaks what he did not say
she's so flat-chested
why would anyone want to rape her

***

i can discuss rape psychology
and how it is far more about
power held over another than
however one defines physical beauty
or i can give the simplest of answers

when has rape ever listened
to rhyme or reason
or anything outside of pure evil
when has rape ever been logical

untitled xv

it matters not how smart
you think you are
nor how smart
i think you to be

if ever someone learns i was raped
and they choose to speak in response
all i ever think is
go ahead
say something stupid

i've never been wrong

mirror poem v

now that the statute of limitations has passed
i shall say everything i have held within

i am sorry i truly am sorry
please believe me

i know
i killed your potential
i killed your purity
i killed you

i'm sorry your soul i stole
i shouldn't have denied it
in court and everywhere else

i wish i wasn't the reason why
you wake up at night
i apologize for i'm still alive
i know you want me dead

do you remember your beloved kanzashi
it's now yours once again
you can finally have back the evidence i hid

i am sorry i truly am sorry
please believe me
please believe me
i am sorry i truly am sorry

you can finally have back the evidence i hid
it's now yours once again
do you remember your beloved kanzashi

i know you want me dead
i apologize for i'm still alive
you wake up at night
i wish i wasn't the reason why

in court and everywhere else
i shouldn't have denied it
i'm sorry your soul i stole

i killed you

i killed your purity
i killed your potential
i know

please believe me
i am sorry i truly am sorry

i shall say everything i have held within
now that the statute of limitations has passed

untitled xvi

you think what i once thought
he hurt me most
but it is he
who authors my torment
whilst it is you
my subconscious gambles not
to think about

i can write him off
as an entity of man's evil
and be done with it
but you you are woman
you are what the little girl
i once was
was going to grow up to be

and you didn't protect me

i've never looked at woman the same
since you

untitled xvii

today i cry my tears spill
and soften the skin
upon my left wrist

in thought i freeze
i'm making tears and i am breathing
i have a soul

and it is mine

untitled xviii

the afternoon my friend told me
he was sexually abused as a child
was the afternoon i learned how to listen

when i weighed his words days later
i could feel our similarities
but him being male and i female
i could more feel our differences

he too was not believed
he too was labeled at fault
he too once doubted
if it was his doing or his molester's
all for different reasons
than i had faced

i cannot write of his life
or more generally
of a male being sexually abused
nor should i

despite knowing men who have
and who have gifted me their words
they let me listen to them
just to listen

we both know my understanding
of their voice and silence
can only go as far as conceptual

i will never understand
their humanity
their strength
their depth
their everything

untitled xix

tell me the truth

the actual truth
or what you'll believe

birthday

to fill a sunday
i attend an art class in the afternoon
the instructor allows us freedom
look around the room
what inanimate object strikes you
paint its curves and edges and enjoy

i note the dull clock on the wall and smile
noting my skill level
i accept the challenge of painting a circle

the second hand doesn't stay still
and is frustrating to paint
i decide my clock will do without one

in rebellion i paint my own time
i set the minute and hour hands
to my best friend's birthday
paint her initials
above the six for design

realizing i have thirty-one minutes
and whatever seconds left in the class
i paint a clock for myself

i set the minute and hour hands
to my birthday
paint my initials
above the six for design
and try not to hyperventilate
you were born
you were born you were born you were born

despite wishing i had been aborted
every day
i am here

my mieko

like a child in a cozy coat
she smiles

iii

sestine xix

i remember us crossing at the dinner the night after
i remember trying to sit up straight
i remember trying not to feel inside
i remember you not noticing my breathing growing short
i remember wishing the phone to ring
i remember i was the only one knowing why

i remember being confused as to why
i could hear after
every sentence a stinging ring

i remember wanting to call yesterday what it was straight
i remember how that turned out when i was a child so short
i remember you had sensed this inside

i remember staring through you to see if you had my soul inside
i remember hoping i could prove why
you could block the sun with your soul and mold darkness wide tall short
i remember you looking so innocent after
every sentence spoken with eye contact so straight

i remember wishing the phone to ring i remember wishing the phone to ring
i remember wishing the phone to ring i remember wishing the phone to ring
i remember already knowing inside
if i told the truth straight
and answered everyone's ignorantly stupid whys
no one would still believe me after
and instead merely wait for my voice to grow small slight short

i remember my wish fell short
and the phone the phone didn't ring
i remember trying to exhale after inhale exhale after inhale exhale after

i remember everything of that noon from the inside
i remember not knowing why
you bent my legs so straight
and entered me so straight
i remember you made sure the pain wasn't short
why

i remember the ring
of me screeching inside
i remember feeling no end in sight no after
i remember why you gave me an after

with straight arms and straight form you finish inside
not a second short of when the phone wrings

untitled xx

my friend comes across a rape whistle
whilst online shopping
apparently this is enough
to have him speak
i'm sick and tired
of men being seen as monsters

i look at him with admiration and envy
what a luxury it is
to solely fear being seen a monster

untitled xxi

you tell me you were raped
and i believe you
i tell you i was raped
you deem it consensual

untitled xxii

she asks if there's anything
she can do to help
i see through her
know she is asking
to feel like a decent person
but not actually asking
for my sake

i want to be honest with her
but can't
i want to say the truth
i need you to step up
be a real friend

since you've not the words nor answers
at minimum gift me your shoulder
so i can weep
weep till your entire sweater changes color
and is darkened by my tears
weep till i'm no longer sure i have eyes

and when that is done
whenever it is done
tuck me in with the softest blanket
this world has ever woven
turn the dial on the dimmer
and simply say
sweet dreams sweetheart

untitled xxiii

the woman to my right at the dinner party
is a police officer by day
or by night depending on her shift

both wanting ice from the freezer
we have a moment alone
by the kitchen counter
pardon me for the odd question
but please tell me
does your precinct take rape seriously

she looks at me knowing
there is only one correct answer
to such a question
but for me it doesn't matter if
she tells the truth or lies

i just need to hear someone
for once in my life
say yes

she was asking for it

if i place a loaded gun in front of you
torque your wrist hard enough
to leave black and blue lines
force you to put the steel to my head
does that then erase your humanity enough
to pull the trigger

either way you answer
is more humane than rape

tears

it takes a village
to raise a child
and a village
to break one

cut pantoum ix

teach me what i say is true only if others believe it
when you didn't believe it was rape you called me a lying slut
teach me who i am till i say what everyone's been waiting for

when you didn't know how i was making a living you called me a prostitute
when you didn't believe it was rape you called me a lying slut
in my pain i wanted to prove you right

when you didn't know how i was making a living you called me a prostitute
when you heard he tried to kill me with the kitchen knife you thought i'd do the same to you
in my pain i wanted to prove you right
there would be no difference made to my self-worth if i did

when you heard he tried to kill me with the kitchen knife you thought i'd do the same to you
what a monster i must be to be one without having yet done anything

there would be no difference made to my self-worth if i did
proving you wrong won't change what you believe me to be
what a monster i must be to be one without having yet done anything
teach me i am born of evil and will give birth to evil

proving you wrong won't change what you believe me to be
looking in the mirror now is always a surprise
teach me i am born of evil and will give birth to evil
lock in my confession

looking in the mirror now is always a surprise
i am a liar a slut a prostitute a monster and any other title you wish to give me
lock in my confession

i wasn't raped i lied

how to get away with rape

1. rape
2.

villanelle vii

when you walk when you wail when you wink when you wonder
there is no way around it
you my friend are a part of rape culture

if you've never met a rapist a molester or a sexual abuse survivor
you're not listening one bit
when you walk when you wail when you wink when you wonder

when you don't know what to say or how to be in our corner
yet speak with the zero research you emit
you my friend are a part of rape culture

you rapist you victim you supporter you not you mere person yonder
shove the millions of ways to say fault and don't believe up your armpit
when you walk when you wail when you wink when you wonder

when you grow numb to supporting us it him or her
and are comfortable using this as a cop-out or quit
you my friend are a part of rape culture

if you believe you stunt not the inhales of survivors and won't in future
it matters not a whit
when you walk when you wail when you wink when you wonder
you my friend are a part of rape culture

for those who wish me wordless

if everyone had just believed me
from the beginning
this book would've been one page
one poem long

afternoon curtains

she keeps them closed
when she doesn't want to remember
but leaves a sliver open for sun
to remind her there's hope

untitled xxiv

i walk into the office
and am noted
wow you look radiant
more beautiful
than you've ever been
what's changed

i believe myself
don't you mean
you believe in yourself

no

iv

villanelle viii

it hurts too much what pain is this
aftermath my dear
there is a way as promised

where is my pulse why is my body remiss
am i dead or is there more to fear
it hurts too much what pain is this

almost all of your life that night will kiss
though relief will not knock near
there is a way as promised

i want to scream but can't breathe in this abyss
my blood has no rufous my tears no clear
it hurts too much what pain is this

trust the stings the screams the stabs will dismiss
though they will never fully they will disappear
there is a way as promised

my stolen soul i miss
please tell me this'll be my darkest tear
it hurts too much what pain is this

there is a way as promised

untitled xxv

mieko wishes not to
go out for ice cream
at her favorite parlor
there are men out there
in the world
what if they rape me

sweetheart look at me
strangers sometimes rape
but more often than not
rape is committed
by someone a person knows

she pauses
okay i want a milkshake instead

untitled xxvi

mieko smiles
for not having had a flashback
in her nightmares last night

proud of her
i clothe her warmth
with my arms and whisper
when you come across
these accomplishments no one sees
know you and survivors you've never met
feel it

untitled xxvii

one day i wake
realize i deserve
to be treated humanely
there should be no abuse

i sit up confused
i've never felt this before
what do i do now

lune xx

it is mieko's
birthday and
i celebrate it

untitled xxviii

my last appointment for the week
is an interview with a man
who's only skimmed my book

before the fourth question
he points out i speak with deep confidence
if he skipped skimming he'd know
i speak without doubt

he asks how i got to be this way
i provide the one-worded answer of training
he asks me to expound
my impressionable years were exposed
to people trying to make me doubt myself
especially trying to gaslight me
on the fact i was abused
i've trained myself every day for years
to listen to the truth my inner voice speaks

simply put it's easy to sound confident
when you know you are speaking of
what is factual and true

now this is a fascinating quality you have
would you say you wouldn't have this
to this degree
if you didn't undergo abuse
correct

he dares move on
asks another question
instead of answering it

i return to his former
you're trying to find a silver lining
the thing about silver linings is
they tend to find a positive by-product
from something tragic
whilst ignoring the tragedy

there are countless beautiful qualities
i've developed from being a survivor
and from continuing to survive
but i'd take not having such qualities
and possibly being a worse person
over the pain that is sexual abuse
any day

i'm sorry if i've offended you
he really should have apologized
for addressing sexual abuse so commonly

we continue with the interview
whilst i wonder what was the point
in writing my book

dizain xxvii

i know what i did conscience is ringing
but who among us would turn himself in
you who have blamed her would do the same thing
as we both know it's not the worst of sins

i don't deserve a ruined life begin
over something that can be forgiven
after all i've stopped at one girl riven
jail is but a merely pointless ordeal

guilt is torment enough i have striven
oh sweet peace i can hear my conscience heal

survivor

what you'll never understand is
by still being able to breathe today
i've accomplished more than you'll ever
in a lifetime

period

you scrape and scrape
the inner top layer
of my womb
till you see blood
i used to hate you
if i'm being honest
some days i still do

though you keep me bedridden
you are lovely
you are my reminder
of how beautiful it is
to be woman to be birther
to be able to birth these words
birth these answers
birth this book
birth the people who read it

to be able to birth the world

untitled xxix

tonight i read in bed
mieko pulls the blanket
over her shoulders
and tucks herself in
to need not say
it's bedtime you owl
put down the pages
turn off the light

i know i should let her sleep
but there's an answer i first need
sweetheart do you see me
as a mother or
as a friend

trying to stay awake
for she is sweeter than i
when you read me your poems
and spit truth
you're a person

how beautiful

i lie with my love
for the first time

so this is what it feels like
with consent

untitled xxx

he asks his third question of the interview
getting in touch with one's inner child
is an important part of the process
but mieko is so prominent in this book
that one might question the oddity of this

i try to conceal my smile
as i note he's done his research
this is going to be a good interview

the moment i fell in love with you

i come home and
mieko's face spells guilt
i scan all that can be broken
and find half of my manuscript
dressing the living room floor

allowing me no breaths
to seek the other half
she makes sure i note
the power her fingers hold

she picks up page eighteen
and dog-ears it
simply because she knows
this makes my eyes scream

unashamed her smile turns to me
what's a petunia

untitled xxxi

mieko and i sit in silence
in our stillness she studies me

she waits for something in particular
then holds my hand with her eyes
you are worthy

i look down to carpet
or whatever is not her
for though these are the words i need
they are so hard to hear

again she waits
till our silence repeats her words

untitled xxxii

i live in a house on a hill
overlooking a small forest
when buying it the selling point
the real estate agent drove home
was that it was on a hill
overlooking a small forest

the window in my study faces west
the forest yonder lies west
i drive down the hill
and through the winding road
hugging the forest every day

when writer's block
reminds me of its torment
i walk down the hill
hike upon the soil
that nourishes the forest
when i am doing everything
when i am doing nothing
the forest lies to the west

the day i finished my book i breathed
i breathed again and again and again
i breathed in all of
the stuffy air in my study
till i decided to open the window

standing west i looked yonder
hey there are trees over there

untitled xxxiii

i tuck mieko into bed
she falls asleep as if
there were never any poems
to write

i kiss her atop her left brow
whisper the only words
she's ever wished for
sleep soundly sweetheart
it's begun

www.ingramcontent.com/pod-product-compliance
Lightning Source LLC
Chambersburg PA
CBHW011957050726
47498CB00012BA/3014